AF432214

THE EXCURSION
A Modern American Retelling

A Poem

By

Peter James Stouffer

Holly, Michigan, United States of America

2026

PREFACE

A RUST BELT PASTORAL

This poem is an act of translation, though not of language. It is a translation of time and place.

The work you are about to read is a modern adaptation of William Wordsworth's 1814 epic, *The Excursion*. Originally set among the rocky fells of the English Lake District, Wordsworth's poem was a response to the anxieties of his age: the industrialization of the countryside, the political fallout of the French Revolution, and the spiritual displacement of the rural poor.

In re-reading Wordsworth, I realized that his nineteenth-century ghosts are haunting my own backyard. The "Ruined Cottage" of 1814 is the foreclosed home in a zombie subdivision of 2008. The "Solitary," a man disillusioned by failed revolutions, is the modern cynic retreating from a polarized society. The search for a spiritual anchor in a shifting world is as urgent now in the American Midwest as it was in Georgian England.

Therefore, I have transposed the scene to Rose Township and the adjacent Village of Holly, Oakland County, Michigan.

ON THE FORM

The reader may ask: Why call this a poem? It lacks the line breaks of verse; it avoids the rhyme schemes of the nineteenth century. Why not simply call it a novella?

I have retained the title of "Poem" because the intent of this work is not horizontal, but vertical. A novel moves horizontally; it asks, "What happens next?" It rushes from plot point to plot point. But this narrative, like the epic it is based on, moves vertically. It asks, "What does this mean?" It halts the narrative entirely to examine the geometry of a spider's web or the depth of a foundation.

Furthermore, the figures you will meet here —Samuel, Elias, Father Tom—are not merely characters in the psychological sense; they are Archetypes. By capitalizing their titles (The Surveyor, The Solitary, The Priest), I intend to signal that they are not just men inhabiting a landscape, but spirits inhabiting a condition. They speak in the rhythm of the oration rather than the chatter of the coffee shop.

THE GEOGRAPHY

The geography of this poem is real. The glacial moraines, the gravel roads, and the struggling villages are those of the Rust Belt. In this retelling, Wordsworth's "Wanderer"—originally a Peddler—

becomes Samuel Walker, a retired Land Surveyor who reads the scripture of the earth through the water table and the stars. The "Solitary" becomes Dr. Elias Thorne, a grieving academic hiding in a fen off Fish Lake Road. The "Pastor" is Father Tom Cole of St. Jude's, keeping the history of the dead in a town that is trying to forget its losses. And the Narrator is Jim Miller, a freelance writer caught in the "Millennial Drift," serving as the witness to their debate.

The poem follows the exact structure of the original nine books:

BOOK I: A meeting at Tipsico Lake and the tragedy of the Ghost Subdivision.

BOOK II–IV: A descent into the Fen to debate the Solitary's nihilism and the "geometry of loss."

BOOK V: A transition from the wild earth to the ordered history of the Village of Holly.

BOOK VI–VII: A walk through Lakeside Cemetery, where the stories of the dead are recounted to prove that no life is truly lost.

BOOK VIII–IX: A return to the living community at "Battle Alley Brews" and a final retreat to a farmhouse on Hensell Road.

This is a "Rust Belt Pastoral." It does not shy away from the decay—the rust, the Tyvek, the invasive weeds—but it insists, as Wordsworth did, that an "active principle" of hope survives. It suggests that our lives are not stagnant pools, but part of a living watershed—a current that endures even the harshest winters.

TABLE OF CONTENTS

BOOK I

THE GHOST SUBDIVISION

"A map is just a piece of paper that lies about where the mud is. You can draw a straight line from here to the horizon, but God didn't pave it, and He certainly didn't cosign the loan."

— **Samuel Walker**,
Surveyor's Log

i. The Turnout at Tipsico Lake

"The sun doesn't charge extra to shine on the poor side of the fence. It takes a hell of a lot of money to be as miserable as the man in that pontoon boat looks."

It was the summer of the drying creeks, when the sun climbed high before the coffee brewed and glared distinct through the humidity—a pale steam rising off the fens and lakes of Rose Township. The northern ridges stood dappled with shadows from the brooding clouds, but down here, by the water, the heat held still.

I pulled my car onto a patch of dust, a gravel easement between the road and the private fence —that strip of "borrowed ground" the township claims but never paves. My phone buzzed in my pocket—another rejection email, or perhaps a Venmo notification for a gig that paid too little, too late. I let it buzz. I was thirty-two, over-educated and under-employed, drifting through the gig economy like a ghost in the machine. I was looking for something solid, and the only solid thing I knew was parked right in front of me.

Samuel Walker sat in a folding chair beside his vintage Airstream. The trailer was dull as a worn-out dime, an aluminum hull docked in the tall grass. He held the shoulder, strictly legal, existing in that liminal strip between the asphalt blur and the cool, private privilege of the lake.

He was seventy-four, a man who had spent his life with a transit level and a chain. He used a digital theodolite now, but he still kept his grandfather Jacob's brass transit in the truck cab—a heavy, purely mechanical talisman from 1920.

He knew the water table better than he knew the parish priest. He read the scripture of the glacial till and the holy text of the moraines. Retired now, he kept his hickory surveyor's pole leaning against the trailer like a shepherd's crook.

"You're late," he said, not looking up. He was watching the light hit Tipsico Lake, glinting off the aluminum docks and the pontoon boats he could see but never own.

"I had to file a story," I lied. I hadn't filed a story in weeks. I was paralyzed by the noise of it all—the constant scroll, the panic of the rent due on the drafty cabin I rented.

Samuel turned. His face was a map of deep lines, tanned by fifty years of working outdoors. He looked at me—pale, anxious, checking my phone again—and his eyes narrowed. He didn't judge, but he measured. That was his trade. He looked for the grade, and he saw I was slipping.

"Sit," he commanded, kicking a spare crate toward me. "The heat is good for the bones. It dries out the nonsense."

We sat in the silence of the roadside. A truck thundered past, rattling the gravel, but Samuel didn't flinch. He was fixed on something else.

"I was thinking," he said, his voice like gravel rolling in a mixer, "about the difference between a ruin and a wreck. A ruin has dignity. A castle, an abbey—they fall, but they leave a shape. But what we build now? The vinyl? The particle board?" He spat into the dust. "It doesn't ruin, Jim. It just rots. It turns to slush."

He pointed with his chin down the road, toward a paved cul-de-sac that ended abruptly in a wall of sumac.

"You know that place?"

"The unfinished sub?" I asked. "The one they stopped building in '08?"

"The Ghost Subdivision," he corrected. "Let's go. I want to show you what happens when the math is wrong."

❧

ii. The Geometry of Loss

"There is no such thing as a 'permanent improvement.' There's just things we built today that the weeds haven't figured out how to eat yet. Give 'em time."

We walked down the hot asphalt of Hickory Ridge to the entrance of the sub. The road was wide, curbed, and guttered, built for fifty luxury homes that never came. The sewer caps were stamped with the date 2007. Grass grew three feet high through the cracks in the pavement. It was a zombie street, a monument to a bubble that burst before the paint was dry.

Only one house stood in the desolation. It was a foreclosure, a two-story colonial with the vinyl siding peeling off the north face like dead skin. The windows were dark. The "For Sale" sign had long since fallen into the weeds, bleached white by winter after winter.

"Maggie's place," Samuel said softly. He stopped at the edge of the driveway, respecting a property line that the bank had long forgotten.

"I knew her," he said. "Maggie Kowalski. She was a nurse's aide. Strong hands. Eyes that were always looking for a reason to laugh, even when there wasn't one. She moved here with her husband, Rob. He was a carpenter. Good with wood, bad with credit. But they had the dream, Jim. They signed the papers. They thought the world was going up and to the right, forever."

Samuel traced a line in the air with his hand, leveling the horizon.

"Rob was a provider. That was his religion. When the crash came, when the developer—Mr. Sterling—went bankrupt and vanished to Florida, the work stopped. The subdivision died overnight. Rob sat on this porch for a month, watching his tools rust. Then he heard about the oil fields in North Dakota. The Bakken. 'Black Gold,' they said. 'Jobs for any man with a pulse and a strong back.'"

"He left on a Monday," Samuel continued. "He kissed Maggie. He kissed the baby. He said, 'I'll send the check in two weeks.' He drove his truck west, chasing the boom."

"And?" I asked, though I knew the rhythm of this story. It was the anthem of the Rust Belt.

"And the checks came for a while," Samuel said. "Then they got smaller. Then they stopped. Then the phone was disconnected. Disappeared. Swallowed by the camps. Maybe it was an accident on the rig. Maybe it was the meth that floats through those oil towns like snow. Maybe he just couldn't bear the shame of coming home empty."

❧

iii. The Waiting

"Hope is a fine breakfast but a lousy supper. A woman can live a long time on bread and water, but she'll starve to death in a week on promises."

Samuel walked up the cracked driveway. He touched the peeling siding, feeling the cheapness of the material.

"She waited," he said. "That was her work. She waited while the weeds took the lawn. She waited while the neighbors walked away from their mortgages. She waited while the baby got sick—some respiratory thing, the damp in the walls, maybe, or just the poverty setting in."

I looked at the house. I tried to imagine it—the silence of the phone, the slow creeping panic as the bank notices piled up like snowdrifts against the door. I felt a cold prickle of recognition. I knew that panic. I felt it every time my lease was up for renewal.

"The baby died in the winter," Samuel said, his voice flat, brutal. "Pneumonia. Or neglect. Or just a lack of heat. Who can say? The county came and took the eldest boy—sent him to an aunt in Flint because there was no food in the cupboard. Maggie didn't fight them. She was already gone.

"She turned into a ghost in her own kitchen. I'd see her sometimes, wandering the county roads in Rob's old flannel jacket. It was three sizes too big, hanging off her wasted frame like a shroud. She'd stop trucks with out-of-state plates. 'Have you been to the Bakken?' she'd ask. 'Have you seen a carpenter named Rob?'"

Samuel turned back to me, his eyes hard and bright.

"She died right here," he pointed to the porch steps, where a colony of ants was dismantling a dead beetle. "Found by the mailman on a Tuesday. Heart failure, the coroner wrote. But that's medical shorthand. She died of waiting, Jim. She died of a subdivision that promised a life it couldn't guarantee."

He kicked a piece of loose siding. It clattered across the cement.

"And now? The bank owns the deed. They'll doze it down come August. Scrape the lot clean. The siding, the drywall, the memories—all into a dumpster. And the woods will creep back in to swallow the scar. In five years, you'll never know a woman loved a man right here, and lost the world for it."

ʠ

iv. The Descent

"A vinyl house is like a politician's smile: shiny, uniform, and hollow in the middle. It'll hold up just fine right until the weather turns."

I looked at the house. It wasn't just a sad story. It was a threat. It was the physical manifestation of my generation's nightmare: the precariousness of it all. One bad year, one lost gig, one shift in the global economy, and the weeds come for you.

"It's all fragile," I whispered. "Everything we build. It's just Tyvek and debt."

Samuel adjusted his cap. He saw the fear in my face—the nihilism creeping in at the edges.

"It is fragile," he agreed. "If you build on the drift. That is why we must go deeper."

He picked up his pole.

"The air is too heavy here. It's full of ghosts. I need to breathe the Fen air to clear my lungs. I'm going to see the Doctor."

"Elias?" I asked. "The Solitary?"

"The man who thinks this," Samuel swept his hand over the ruined lawn, "is the only truth. He lives in the muck because he thinks the muck is honest. He thinks despair is the only logical response to a world that kills babies and forecloses on widows."

Samuel looked at me, a challenge in his eyes.

"You're scared, Jim. I can see it. You look at this house and you see your own future. You think the system is rigged and the rot is inevitable."

I didn't answer. He was right.

"Come with me," Samuel said, starting back toward the truck. "Let's go talk to the man who gave up. Let's hear his argument. Because unless you can answer him, unless you can find a reason to build on this shifting ground... you'll end up just like him."

I looked at the house one last time—the empty windows staring like skull sockets—and then I followed him. I wasn't going for the scenery. I was going because I needed to know if there was an alternative to the rot.

"Lead on, Surveyor," I said. "Take me to the swamp."

BOOK II

THE FEN

"Civilization is just a layer of blacktop we pour over the mud so we don't have to look at where we came from. But the mud is patient. It knows the road is just renting the space."

— Samuel Walker,
Hydrology Reports, Vol. 4

i. The Green Tunnel

"If you need a satellite to tell you that you are stand-ing in a swamp, you were lost long before the signal died."

We left the pavement where the dream had died and turned the truck onto a two-track lane that vanished into walls of green. The transition was violent. One moment, we were in the open glare of the foreclosure; the next, we were swallowed by the canopy of Fish Lake Road.

The air changed instantly. The dry, dusty heat of the subdivision broke, replaced by something heavy, mineral, and cold—a smell of calcium, rotting peat, and moisture hanging in the air.

"Not a swamp," Samuel said, cutting the wheel to dodge a crater in the sandy track. He spoke defensively, as if the land were a misunderstood relative. "A swamp is fed by rain and river flood. It's surface water. This... this is a Fen. It drinks from the deep earth. The water here pushes up from the aquifers, filtering through the gravel and the lime until it makes a soup that preserves the bone and dissolves the boot."

We parked where the ground grew too soft to drive, beside a stand of Tamaracks—those strange, deciduous conifers that turn a smoky gold before they drop their needles. Now they were green, feathery, and soft, rising like spires above the sedge meadow.

I stepped out of the truck and immediately felt the ground give way. It wasn't mud; it was a sponge. The earth breathed under my weight.

"Watch where you step," Samuel warned, grabbing his hickory pole. He paused by a massive White Oak at the edge of the path. It was a deformity of nature—the trunk grew straight, took a violent ninety-degree turn, ran horizontal for two feet, and then shot up again. A perfect Z-shape scarring the woods.

"Indian marker tree," Samuel grunted, patting the horizontal limb. "Or maybe just a bored farm boy a hundred years ago trying to write his name on the world. Either way, it points to the dry ground."

"The mats look solid, but the peat is deep. You step on a hummock, you stay dry. You step between them? You'll be waist-deep in a thousand years of decomposed grass."

I looked at the path ahead. It was a tunnel of invasive phragmites, the reeds towering twelve feet high, blocking out the sky, the horizon, and the cell service. I checked my phone. No Signal.

A wave of relief washed over me, followed immediately by guilt. The noise of the world—the emails, the invoices, the news cycle—couldn't follow me here. I understood, in a dangerous flash, why a man might choose to hide in a hole like this.

ii. The Sinking Cabin

"A house is like a reputation: it takes years to build and about one rainy season to ruin. If you stop shimming the floorboards, you aren't making a philosophical statement. You're just making a compost pile."

We walked single file, Samuel leading like a pilgrim, me following like a tourist in hell. The alternating cool and heat here was wet, steaming off the tussocks of wiregrass. Shrubby cinquefoil bloomed in yellow bursts, and sumac, with its red-stemmed fruit, stood beautiful and toxic on the fringe.

And then, the house appeared.

It was a hunting shack from the late 1940s, a square of asphalt siding that had once been faux-brick red but was now the color of a bruise. It sat —or rather, floated—on a slight rise in the center of the marsh. The porch listed heavily to the left. The steps had already surrendered to the muck.

"He's letting it go," Samuel whispered, stopping at the edge of the clearing. He pointed to the corner post, where a stack of slate shards—carefully placed eighty years ago to level the floor—had slipped into the muck. "He refuses to shim the foundation. He says he wants to see how long it takes for the earth to take it back."

Samuel tapped the rotting railing with his hickory pole, listening to the hollow thud.

"You know who built this? Ben East."

I looked at the ruin with new respect. "The naturalist? The editor for *Outdoor Life*?"

"The very same," Samuel said. "Born right here in Rose. Before he became the 'Dean of Outdoor Writers' and went off to ghostwrite stories about bear attacks in Alaska, he used to come back here to listen to the silence. He framed this shack himself in '48. He wanted a place where the only deadline was the sunset."

Samuel shook his head.

"Ben East spent his life writing about men who survived the wilderness—about 'Narrow Escapes' and the will to live. And now? Elias sits inside the great man's cabin, writing the exact opposite."

"What's he writing?" I asked.

"Nothing," Samuel said. "He's editing the sequel. The Great Surrender."

On the porch, a figure sat in a recliner that was losing its stuffing. Dr. Elias Thorne.

He didn't look like a professor. He looked like a castaway. He wore a flannel shirt that had been washed until it was transparent, and his beard was a gray thicket that mirrored the brush around him. He was watching a spider weave a web between the porch railing and a handle of a whiskey jug.

He didn't move as we approached. He didn't wave. He just watched the spider.

"The geometry is perfect," Elias said, his voice rusty, as if he hadn't used it in days. "Look at the tension. She builds the web every night. The wind destroys it every morning. She builds it again. She has no memory of the failure. That is her advantage over us, Samuel."

He finally looked up. His eyes were startlingly clear, blue and sharp, the only part of him that hadn't gone to seed. He looked at Samuel, then he looked at me. He saw the notebook in my pocket. He saw the clean boots. He saw the hesitation.

"And who is this?" Elias asked. "A disciple? Or just another witness to the decline?"

"This is Jim," Samuel said, stepping onto the porch. The wood groaned under his boot. "He's writing a story about the county. I told him you were the only man who knew the bottom of it."

Elias laughed. It was a dry, hacking sound. "The bottom? There is no bottom, Jim. That's the joke. But come in. The mosquitoes are starting their shift. They are the only reliable workforce left in Michigan."

❧

iii. The Museum of Abandonment

"You can pile up all the philosophy books you want, but they make a poor dam. Water reads faster than a professor, and it always gets the last word."

The inside of the cabin was a shock. I expected squalor—hoarded newspapers, dirty plates, the madness of a recluse.

Instead, I found a library.

Books were stacked everywhere. Not on shelves—the shelves had rotted away—but in towers on the floor. Pillars of philosophy, political science, and history rose from the linoleum like stalagmites. *Leviathan. The Social Contract. A Theory of Justice.*

But the room was dying. The wallpaper was peeling in long, damp strips. A bucket in the corner caught a rhythmic drip-drip-drip from the ceiling, the water dark with tannin. The smell was overwhelming—old paper, stale rye, and the sweet, cloying scent of mold.

"Sit," Elias commanded, pointing to a wooden crate. "Don't lean back. The wall is soft."

He moved to a kitchenette—a museum piece from the Eisenhower era—and measured out three shots of amber liquid. No ice.

On the small table lay a single object that seemed out of place among the rotting philosophy texts. It was a thick manuscript, hand-bound, the cover stained with water and age. The title was handwritten in a script that spoke of 1920s precision: *The Witness.*

Elias saw me eyeing it. He placed his hand on the cover, a protective gesture—odd for a man who claimed to value nothing.

"Rye," he said. "Cheap. Burns the throat, clears the sinuses."

He handed me a glass. I took it, afraid to refuse.

"You are a 'Writer,'" Elias said, settling back into his ruin of a chair. "A Gig Economy worker. A Millennial drifter."

He said the words with a surgical precision, dissecting my life before I'd even spoken.

"I'm a freelancer," I said, my voice sounding thin in the damp room. "I observe."

"You drift," Elias corrected. "You float on the surface tension of the economy, waiting for a bubble to burst. You are like the water striders out there. You skate on top, terrified of breaking the film and falling in."

He took a long drink, his eyes fixing on Samuel.

"Samuel here," he gestured with the glass, "is a Surveyor. He believes in the Grid. He believes that if you drive a stake deep enough, you hit something solid. He thinks this..." he waved at the rotting walls, "...is just a temporary error. A glitch in the divine program."

"It is a season," Samuel said calmly, resting his hands on his knees. "Winter comes. Winter goes. The root survives."

"Does it?" Elias leaned forward. The shadows from the window bars fell across his face like cage wires. "Or does the root just rot slower than the leaf?"

&

iv. The Subtraction

"The Doctor thinks if he strips his life down, he'll find a diamond in the middle. But a man isn't a rock; he's an onion. You peel off enough layers, you don't find a prize—you just find yourself crying over a handful of nothing."

"You look at this place," Elias said to me, "and you see a tragedy. You see a man who has 'let himself go.' That is the phrase, isn't it? 'He really let himself go.'"

He smiled, and it was terrifying.

"But you are wrong, Jim. This isn't a tragedy. It is an experiment. I am a scientist. I am testing a hypothesis: How much can a man subtract from his existence before he hits zero?"

He held up one finger.

"I have subtracted the Career. I was a Professor. I stood in lecture halls in Ann Arbor and taught three hundred children that the system works. I drew diagrams of Checks and Balances. I promised them that if they voted and paid taxes, the Social Contract would protect them."

He lowered the finger.

"Then a drunk driver on I-75 subtracted my wife. And my two children. In a single second, the

Social Contract was voided. The system did not protect them. The pavement did not care. The law could not put the blood back in their veins."

He held up another finger.

"So I subtracted the Faith. Then I subtracted the Ambition. Then I subtracted the House, the Lawn, the Neighbors, the Voting Booth, the Internet."

He gestured to the sinking room.

"I have stripped it all away. I am down to the bone. I am waiting to see if there is a 'Core' that remains. If there is a 'Soul' that shines in the dark."

He looked at his glass, swirling the cheap whiskey.

"And do you know what I have found, Jim? In the silence? In the dark?"

I couldn't breathe. The air in the cabin was too thick. "What?" I whispered.

"Nothing," Elias said softly. "I have found that the zero is lower than we think. I have found that a man is just a bundle of habits and anxieties, and when you strip them away... there is just a biological machine, waiting to rust."

He looked at me, and I felt a cold chill that had nothing to do with the damp.

"And you know it," he said. "That is why you are here. You are tired of treading water. You want to know if it's peaceful at the bottom."

Samuel stood up abruptly. The motion broke the spell.

"The bottom is solid," Samuel said, his voice hard. "You just haven't hit it yet because you are too busy admiring the fall."

Samuel walked to the window and wiped the grime from the glass, revealing the green chaos outside.

"You have subtracted everything, Elias. Except your vanity. You are so proud of your despair. But you are still breathing. You are still drinking rye. You are still watching the spider. You are still here."

Samuel turned back to us, the Surveyor taking charge of the line.

"Drink up, Jim. The Professor has given his opening statement. But the trial isn't over. We have a long night ahead."

BOOK III

THE NIHILIST'S SERMON

"A man can preach that the world is pure chaos, but still stacks his books in straight piles. If he really believed in the void, he wouldn't be so worried about keeping it tidy."

— **Samuel Walker**,
Surveyor's Log

i. The Tenure of the Swamp

"We file our deeds in courthouses made of stone, forgetting the stone rests on clay. When the ground shifts, the paper doesn't mean a thing. But that doesn't make the law a lie; it just means the court-room is moving."

The whiskey bottle stood between the three of us, a golden pillar in the gathering dark. The only light came from the steady hiss of a kerosene lantern that Elias had lit against the gloom. It cast long, wavering shadows against the peeling wall-paper, turning the stacks of water-damaged books into a skyline of ruined cities.

Elias spun his glass on the table. He didn't look like a madman now. He looked like a profes-sor holding office hours in hell.

"You are young, Jim," he began, his voice dropping into a register that commanded atten-tion—the muscle memory of twenty years in the lecture hall. "You are still looking for the 'Code.' You think that if you work hard, if you recycle, if you vote, if you are kind, the universe will honor the contract."

He laughed, a dry sound like oak leaves skittering on pavement.

"I taught that contract. I stood in the amphitheaters of Ann Arbor, wearing a tweed jacket that smelled of pipe tobacco and confidence. I drew diagrams on the chalkboard: Input + Effort = Justice. I taught three hundred students a semester that Civilization was a fortress built to keep the Chaos out."

He took a sip of the rye, wincing as it hit his throat.

"I was a priest of the Rational Order. I believed that the institutions—the courts, the banks, the tenure tracks—were real. I thought they were made of granite."

Suddenly, a loud crack echoed through the room. The floorboards beneath my crate lurched a full inch, tilting me toward the center of the room. I grabbed the table to steady myself.

Elias didn't blink. He just pointed a shaking finger at the rotting window frame.

"But they aren't granite. They are Sheetrock. And gravity," he tapped the table, "is the only law that never gets repealed. The house settles. The foundation cracks. The swamp waits."

❧

ii. The Broken Covenant

"An actuary can tell you exactly what a left arm is worth in dollars, but he can't put a price on the silence that fills a kitchen when the front door stops opening. That is a kind of math that breaks the calculator."

"I remember the day it broke," Elias said. He wasn't looking at us anymore; he was looking through the wall, back to a specific stretch of I-75.

"It wasn't the crash itself. Crashes happen. Physics is indifferent to love. No, it was what came after. It was the insurance actuary explaining the 'replacement value' of a seven-year-old girl. It was the drunk driver getting out in eighteen months because of a procedural error in the discovery phase. It was the university suggesting I take a 'sabbatical' because my grief was making the department uncomfortable at mixer events."

He turned his eyes to me. They were sharp, blue, and terrifyingly lucid. He began to dismantle me.

"You feel it, don't you, Jim? The fraud of it?"

I tried to look away, but I couldn't. He was reading my mail.

"You work your 'gigs.' You pay your taxes. You file your invoices. But you know, deep down, that the pension funds have been raided. You know the water pipes in Flint were poisoned to save a decimal point in a budget. You know that if you get sick, an algorithm will decide if you are worth the cost of the pill."

I shifted on my crate, the wood damp against my jeans. I wanted to argue. I wanted to tell him about resilience, about the human spirit. But the words died in my throat because he was right. He was articulating the background hum of my entire adult life—the feeling that the safety net had been sold for scrap metal years ago.

"There is no Social Contract," Elias whispered. "There is only a truce. And the truce is ending."

⣮

iii. The Anatomy of Decay

"A weed cracking the pavement isn't making a statement about the fall of civilization. It's just chasing the sun. You look at the rot and see a sermon, but nature is too busy eating to preach."

Samuel had been silent, his hands folded on the head of his hickory staff. He let the storm blow. He knew you couldn't stop a man like Elias when the pressure valve was open.

"So," Samuel said, his voice calm, "you resigned. You sold the house. You came here to pout among the phragmites."

"I came here to be honest!" Elias snapped. He stood up, pacing the small room. With every step, the floor groaned, a wet, sucking sound that reminded me we were floating on a sponge.

"Look at this place, Samuel. It is disgusting. It is wet. It smells of rot. But it is true. The swamp doesn't lie to you. The mosquito doesn't pretend to be your friend before it takes your blood. The frost doesn't care about your tenure."

He gestured violently at the dark window.

"Out there, the Poweshiek skipperling is going extinct. Not because it 'sinned,' but because it is weak and the habitat changed. The ash trees are dying because the borer beetle is hungry. It is pure. It is a biological machine doing exactly what it was designed to do: consume, reproduce, die."

The wind picked up outside, rattling the loose siding. The whole cabin seemed to sigh, settling deeper into the muck.

"I prefer the cruelty of the Fen to the hypocrisy of the Village," Elias said, leaning over the table, his breath smelling of rye and decay. "At least here, when I sink, the mud doesn't tell me it's for my own good."

❧

iv. The Seduction of Zero

"The whole world is conspiring to lay you flat and cool you off. Standing up is an act of insurrection. Falling down isn't a philosophy; it's just letting gravity do your thinking for you."

I looked at Elias, and for a terrifying moment, I didn't see a monster. I saw a prophet.

The exhaustion hit me all at once. The exhaustion of the hustle. The exhaustion of the rent checks. The exhaustion of hope.

It was so tempting to agree with him. To just stop.

"It's peaceful, isn't it?" Elias said, his voice dropping to a hypnotic softness. "To realize that you don't have to fix it. You can't fix it. The house is burning, Jim. Why run around with a bucket of water? Why not just sit on the porch and watch the sparks? They are quite beautiful, if you stop caring about the house."

He pushed the bottle toward me. The amber liquid caught the light of the lantern.

"Drink up," he whispered. "The first step to freedom is admitting that the game is rigged."

I reached for the glass. My hand was shaking. I looked at the empty corner of the room, where the shadows were deepest. I could imagine a cot there. I could imagine sleeping for a month— letting the phone battery die, the emails bounce, the world deliquescing into the honest, quiet dark.

It felt like gravity. It felt like coming home.

"Let it go, Jim," Elias said. "Join the subtraction. It is the only math that holds up."

❧

v. The Surveyor's Interruption

"If you really believe nothing matters, you stop arguing about it. The fact that you're still shouting at the dark proves you aren't in love with the void—you're just lonely. And loneliness is proof of life."

Clack. Samuel brought his hickory staff down hard on the linoleum. The sound cracked the air like a gunshot, shattering the trance.

"That is enough," Samuel said.

He didn't shout. He didn't have to. He spoke with the authority of a man who had walked ten thousand miles of property lines and knew exactly where the boundaries were.

"You are a brilliant man, Elias," Samuel said, standing up. "And you are using that brilliance to build a very elaborate trap for yourself. You have constructed a perfect logic to justify your cowardice."

"Cowardice?" Elias bristled, the Professor offended. "I am facing the void!"

"Cowardice," Samuel repeated. "It takes no courage to burn the house down. Any fool with a match can do that. It takes courage to fix the roof when it's raining."

Samuel walked to the door and threw it open. The night air rushed in, smelling of wet earth and potential rain, clearing the stale metaphysical smoke of the room.

"You have shown us the Zero, Doctor. You have made your case for the rot. But you have forgotten one thing."

"And what is that?" Elias sneered.

"You forgot that you are still arguing," Samuel said. "If you truly believed it didn't matter, you wouldn't be trying so hard to convince this boy to join you in the dark. You are lonely, Elias. And loneliness is a sign of life."

Samuel turned to me. He saw how close I had come to the edge. He saw that I was still holding the glass.

"Don't drink the Kool-Aid, Jim. It's just cheap rye. We're staying the night. But tomorrow, we are going to show the Professor that the math is bigger than his subtraction."

I looked at the glass. Then I looked at the open door, where the wind was blowing in. I set the glass down.

"Tomorrow," I said. But my voice was weak.

&

BOOK IV

THE SURVEYOR'S REPLY

"Feelings are like topsoil—great for growing weeds, terrible for holding up a roof. If you don't dig down to something that breaks your shovel, you aren't building a house; you're just camping."

— **Samuel Walker**,
Field Notes on Structural Integrity

i. The Iron Pin

"A fence is just a rumor started by a neighbor with a bad memory. The truth is usually buried three feet down, rusty as heck, and stubborn as a mule."

The silence in the cabin was heavy, broken only by the hiss of the lantern and the chaotic rhythm of the frogs outside—a million biological machines screaming for mates in the dark.

Elias sat back, smug in his destruction. He had dismantled the world for us. He had shown us the rot in the walls and the void in the sky. He waited for Samuel to offer a platitude, a Bible verse, something soft that he could tear apart with his razor-sharp despair.

But Samuel didn't offer soft things. He was a Surveyor. He dealt in hard angles and buried steel.

"You have drawn a very convincing map, Doctor," Samuel said, his voice low and vibrating like a cello string. "You have charted the topography of the Fen perfectly. You have measured the depth of the mud. You have calculated the erosion rates of the social contract."

Samuel leaned forward, his hands clasped over the head of his hickory staff.

"But you are making the rookie mistake. You are confusing the Drift with the Deed."

Elias raised an eyebrow. "Enlighten me, Surveyor."

"I spent forty years finding lines that no one could see," Samuel continued. "I'd go out to a farm where the fences had moved, the river had changed course, and the owner swore he owned up to the oak tree. But the oak tree is surface. The fence is surface. They move. They rot. They lie."

"I didn't look for the fence. I dug. I dug through the poison ivy and the clay until I hit the Section Corner. An iron pipe, driven five feet down in the twenties to replace the rotting white oak post set by the state engineers in the 1830s. It was rusted, yes. But it hadn't moved an inch. The grid holds true, Elias. Even when the surface turns to slush."

❧

ii. The Discipline of Hope

"Optimism is betting the roof won't leak. Hope is climbing the ladder in the rain to patch the shingle. One makes you smile; the other keeps you dry."

"That is a lovely metaphor," Elias scoffed, reaching for the empty bottle. "But we are talking about dead children and corrupt banks. Where is the 'Iron Pipe' in a world where a drunk driver can erase a family?"

"The Iron Pipe," Samuel said, "is the refusal to let the chaos have the final word."

Samuel stood up. In the small cabin, he seemed to take up all the oxygen.

"You think Hope is a feeling," Samuel said, looking down at the Professor. "You think it's a warm fuzz in the chest, or a naive optimism that 'things will work out.' That is not Hope. That is wishful thinking. And you are right to loathe it."

He pointed the staff at Elias.

"Hope is not an emotion. Hope is a discipline. It is the stubborn, grinding work of locating the coordinates of dignity in the middle of the disaster. It is the widow who packs six lunches when she wants to curl up and die. It is the man who rebuilds the porch even though he knows the snow will crush it again in ten years."

"We don't build because the wood lasts forever," Samuel said. "We build because the act of building defies the rot. That is the Section Corner. It is the choice to impose Order on the entropy, simply because we can."

Samuel leaned back, his eyes drifting toward the east, as if he could see through the dark walls of the cabin to the history buried beneath the township.

"Take Old JC Garner," Samuel said, his voice dropping to a reverent rumble. "He was one of the first to drive a stake in this dirt. Came here with a big dream to dam the Buckhorn, build a mill pond, and grind grain for a city that hadn't been built yet. The plan failed. The mill never turned a wheel. But did he leave? No. He clawed an existence out of the disappointment. He built a home instead. He raised a family that held that one spot of ground for four generations—a hundred and twenty years of refusing to drift. He couldn't conquer the river, Elias, but he conquered the urge to quit. That is the discipline."

❧

iii. The Cold Light

"A nightmare always looks like a prophecy at 3:00 a.m. But ghosts and bad philosophy have the same weakness: neither one can survive a cup of strong coffee and the morning sun."

I sat on my crate, wiping the moisture from my neck. The damp of the Fen had seeped through my jacket. Elias's nihilism, which had felt so warm and seductive an hour ago, now felt like the room itself: stale, wet, and smelling of mildew.

I looked at Elias. He wasn't the strong, tragic hero anymore. He was just a man sweating in a dirty shirt, hoarding his pain like a treasure.

"You are shaking, Jim," Samuel said, noticing my tremor. "The 'Truth' of the swamp has a way of unsettling the blood around 3:00 a.m."

Samuel turned back to Elias.

"I am not asking you to believe in God tonight, Elias. I am not even asking you to believe in the future. I am asking you to conduct a field test."

"A test?" Elias asked, wary.

"You claim the system is zero. You claim the 'Social Contract' is void. I say you are working with outdated data. I say you are sitting in this hole, extrapolating the state of the world from a sample size of one."

Samuel kicked the door open wider. The first gray suggestion of dawn was touching the tops of the dead ash trees.

"Come with us to Holly. Come to the Village. Not to pray—I know you won't bend your knee. But come as a scientist. Observe the specimens. Look at the people in the cemetery. Look at the people in the coffee shop. Test your hypothesis against the reality of their lives."

❧

iv. The Challenge

"You can't survey the county from the bottom of a well. Down there, the only thing you see is a circle of sky, and you start thinking the whole world is empty."

❦

Elias stared at the open door. The morning air rushed in, smelling of mist and wet earth. It was distinct from the stale air of the cabin.

"You want me to go to St. Jude's," Elias sneered. "To see Father Tom. To hear him sanitize the tragedy with incense."

"I want you to see if your 'Zero' holds up in the light," Samuel countered. "Or are you afraid that your beautiful, perfect despair might evaporate if you actually have to look a neighbor in the eye?"

It was the insult that did it. The accusation of intellectual cowardice.

Elias slammed his hand on the table. The dust jumped.

"Fine," he snapped. He stood up, his joints popping, his face gray with exhaustion. "I will come. Not because I believe in your 'Grid,' Samuel. But because I need to prove to you that the rot is universal. We will go to your precious

Village. We will look at your 'Good Citizens.' And I will show you that they are just as broken as I am —they just hide it better under the vinyl siding."

"Fair terms," Samuel said, a slight smile touching his lips. "Grab your coat, Professor. The survey crew is moving out."

§

v. The Exit

"You can argue with the compass until you're blue in the face, but North isn't going to change its mind. Eventually, you've got to shut up and walk."

Elias moved around the cabin, lowering the wick on the lantern until the flame died. The sudden darkness made the smell of the swamp seem heavier.

He paused by the bookshelf, his hand hovering over a water-damaged copy of *The Republic*. His fingers twitched, wanting the weight of the logic, the safety of the argument. He stood there for a long moment, the Academic reaching for his armor.

Then, he dropped his hand. He left the book on the stack.

He grabbed a canvas field jacket, stained with oil and mud, and put it on. He looked like a bear waking from a bad hibernation.

"You realize," Elias grumbled as we stepped onto the sinking porch, "that this changes nothing. I am merely a captive observer."

"Noted," I said, speaking for the first time in hours. My voice was shaky, but my legs were moving. I wanted out of the swamp. I wanted pavement. I wanted to see something that wasn't dying.

We walked single file back through the tunnel of phragmites. The birds were starting to sing —a chaotic, screeching chorus.

"Noise," Elias muttered, swiping at a reed.

"Music," Samuel corrected, marching ahead.

I followed them both, watching their silhouettes against the graying sky—the man who saw the mud and the man who saw the map—praying that Samuel's grid was real enough to hold us all up.

BOOK V

THE PASTOR

"Civilization is mostly just the polite agreement to pave over the mud. It makes the driving smoother, but it doesn't stop the earth from itching underneath."

— **Samuel Walker,**
Surveyor's Log

i. The Ascent from the Fen

"You look at those wires and see a scar on the sky. I see a copper thread stitching the county together. Without it, we are just a bunch of hermits shouting at the trees."

The morning broke gray and hard.

We were in the truck now, escaping the gravity of the swamp. I sat in the middle of the bench seat, wedged between the two old men. Samuel drove with his usual aggression, rattling us down the sandy two-track of Fish Lake Road while sumac branches whipped the side mirrors.

The air inside the cab still smelled of peat and wet wool, but ahead of us, the world was changing.

Hummmmm.

The tires hit the pavement of Grange Hall Road. The sudden hush of the suspension was jarring. We had crossed the invisible border between the wild, indifferent earth and the engineered world of men.

Elias sat by the window, gripping the dashboard with empty hands. He looked out at the passing world: the mailboxes standing like sentries, the mowed lawns, and the power lines draping from pole to pole in perfect catenary curves.

"Gridlines," Elias muttered, eyeing the telephone wires with suspicion. "Illusions of connectivity."

"Infrastructure," Samuel corrected, shifting into overdrive. "Evidence that we are not alone."

We crested the ridge at Groveland, and there it was: The Village of Holly. It lay in the bowl of the hills, a cluster of brick and vinyl, red lights and green lawns. The water tower hovered above it like a tethered moon, marking the center of gravity for every farmer and drifter in the township.

❧

ii. The Citadel of Stone

"You build with wood if you want to be comfortable. You build with stone if you want to be stubborn. That church wasn't built to be pretty; it was built to win an argument with the winter."

We parked behind St. Jude's. It was not a cathedral. It was a workingman's church, built in the 1880s by Irish railroaders who wanted a fortress against the Michigan winter. The stones were fieldstones, hauled from the glacier-scarred fields by horses, piled thick and mortared tight.

Contrasted with Elias's cabin—which was sinking, peeling, and dying—the church looked aggressive in its permanence. It was a heavy, stubborn assertion that we are here and we are staying.

"It looks like a fortress," I observed.

"It is," Samuel said, shutting the truck door. "It holds the line against amnesia. Out here, Jim, if you don't write things down, the woods take them back. This building is the ledger."

Elias stood on the sidewalk, looking at the stained glass windows protected by wire mesh. He looked small against the masonry. He pulled his coat tighter, though the day was warming up.

He was a creature of the shadows exposed to the streetlights.

꿈

iii. The Keeper of the Ledger

"There's two books in every town: the bank ledger and the parish registry. One tells you who paid their bills, and the other tells you who paid the price."

We found Father Tom Cole in the sacristy, but he wasn't praying. He was wrestling with a stuck drawer in a massive oak vestment cabinet.

He was sixty-two, with the build of a man who had played linebacker in high school and never quite lost the shoulders. He wore a black clerics shirt, but the collar was unbuttoned, and his sleeves were rolled up, revealing forearms dusted with wood polish.

"Confounded humidity," he grunted, giving the drawer a final, violent yank. It slid open. He looked up, flushing slightly, then grinned. It was a wide, easy grin—the face of a man who had heard every sin in the county and decided none of them were original enough to be shocked by.

"Samuel!" he boomed. "And you've brought strays."

"I brought a control group," Samuel said, leaning his hickory pole against the wall. "Father, this is Jim, a scribe. And this..."

Father Tom stopped. He looked at Elias. He didn't see the dirt, or the beard, or the smell of cheap rye. He saw the grief. It was his trade to spot it, the way a doctor spots a limp.

"Dr. Thorne," the Priest said, extending a hand. "I haven't seen you since the funeral."

Elias hesitated. He looked at the Priest's hand as if it were a weapon. Then, relying on the reflex of old manners, he took it.

"I am just observing, Reverend," Elias said stiffly. "Samuel believes that a tour of your facility will cure me of my rationality."

"Unlikely," Father Tom laughed. "This place is full of mysteries, not answers. But you are welcome. The coffee is terrible, but the roof doesn't leak."

❧

iv. The Geography of Memory

"We put iron fences around graveyards to make the living feel safer, not to keep the dead in. A ghost doesn't care much about a rusted hinge."

"We aren't here for coffee," Samuel said. "We are here for the Hill."

Father Tom nodded. His demeanor shifted instantly. The jovial maintenance man vanished, and the Pastor appeared. He reached for a ring of brass keys hanging by the vestment case.

"The Hull is here," Father Tom said, resting his palm against the sweating limestone of the sacristy wall. "The ribs, the rivets, the ballast that keeps us upright in the gale. This building is just the displacement, Elias—the thing that pushes back against the chaos to create a dry space."

He walked to the back of the sacristy, to a heavy, arched door made of dark oak, banded with iron. It was a door that looked like it hadn't been opened in a month.

"But a ship exists for its freight, not its paint," the Priest said. "The Cargo—the manifest of souls we've carried through the storm and finally offloaded at the pier? That is out there."

He inserted a long, skeletal key into the lock. The mechanism tumbled with a heavy, resonant clunk—the sound of a vault unsealing.

"This is the Processional Door," Father Tom explained, his hand on the brass latch. "We only open this for the pallbearers. Usually, the guest of honor leaves this room feet first and doesn't come back."

He pushed the heavy wood outward. Sunlight, blinding and white, spilled into the dim sacristy, carrying the scent of cut grass and damp earth.

"But today," the Priest said, stepping into the frame, "we go out on our own two feet. We go to visit the alumni."

We followed him out of the cool stone darkness and into the heat of the day, walking the short path that led from the sanctuary of the living to the iron perimeter of the dead.

꧁

BOOK VI

THE CEMETERY CHRONICLES

"A headstone is a man's final attempt to win an argument with time. He loses, of course, but the rock puts up a good fight."

— **Samuel Walker**, *Field Notes on Municipal History*

i. The Archive of Stone

"Ink fades and paper burns. If you want to leave a receipt that says you existed, you better carve it in something that breaks a shovel."

The iron gates of Lakeside Cemetery guarded the bluff, severing the asphalt of the village from the green, suspended time of the hill.

They were tall, wrought-iron sentries, rusted to the color of dried paprika.

"You call this 'Order,'" Elias sneered, stopping at the threshold. He pointed through the bars to the rows of stones. "I call it a landfill. It is a sanitary disposal site for biology. You put the calcium in a box, you bury it below the frost line, and you pretend that the name on the rock means the person is still there."

"They are not there," Father Tom said softly.

The Priest reached out and pushed the gate.

Groaaan.

The hinges screamed—a high, metal-on-metal cry like a heavy book spine cracking after years of disuse. It was the sound of iron waking up.

"The bodies are seeds, Doctor. But the names... the names are the map. You say the system is zero? You say the social contract is void?"

Father Tom swept his hand across the acres of granite revealed as the gates swung wide.

"Every stone here is a contract. A promise that someone lived, someone was loved, and someone was left behind to pay the bill for the carving. This isn't a landfill. It is a library. And I know every story in the stacks."

He stepped through the open gates.

"Come," the Priest said. "Let me introduce you to the congregation that doesn't leave."

Elias looked at Samuel. Samuel nodded. We followed the Priest into the city of the dead, leaving the noise of the living village behind us.

The air here was different—still, filtered through the canopy of massive oaks that had witnessed the passing of the carriage, the Model T, and the SUV. The stones ranged from the illegible white tablets of the 1840s, softening like bars of soap, to the laser-etched granite of last week, sharp and black as smartphone screens.

We walked deep into the older section, where the moss claimed the names, before circling back to the newer plots near the edge of the bluff. Here, the earth was still settling.

❧

ii. The Aperture (Ethan)

"Most of us walk through life in steel-toed boots; we don't feel the kick. But the artist walks barefoot. Every pebble is a knife. You can't blame a man for seeking a little anesthesia when the road is made of glass."

Father Tom stopped at a headstone that was stark in its modernity. It featured an etching of a camera on a tripod. The birth date was 1998. The death date was three years ago.

"Ethan," the Priest said softly. "You would have liked him, Elias. He was a 'Noticer.' While the other boys were playing football, he was lying in the wet grass, waiting for the light to hit a dragonfly's wing just right."

"A photographer?" I asked.

"An artist," the Priest said. "He was porous. That was his gift and his curse. The world entered him without a filter. He saw the beauty that we walk past, but he felt the ugly, too. He felt the rust and the gray sky like a physical weight."

"He loved a girl," Samuel added, looking at the horizon. "Rachel. The Valedictorian. Sharp as a tack and ambitious as a strip mall developer."

"She left," Father Tom continued. "She went to Chicago. Marketing. Branding. The hustle. She wanted a life that moved fast. Ethan... he wanted a life that stood still. When she left, the silence she left behind was too loud for him."

Elias looked at the stone. "So he died of a broken heart? A Romantic cliché."

"He died of fentanyl," Father Tom said, the word cutting through the summer air like a knife. "He shattered his ankle hiking. The doctor gave him a script. And he found that the pills did what the camera couldn't—they stopped the aperture down. They made the world less bright, less loud, less sharp. They turned the focus off."

"We found him in his darkroom," the Priest said. "Surrounded by his prints. Beautiful pictures of dead factories and winter fields. He had finally achieved the perfect stillness."

Elias didn't sneer. He looked at the camera etched in the stone. He understood the desire to turn the focus off.

❧

iii. The Alchemist of Scrap (Silas)

"A fool looks at a rusted Chevy and sees trash. A wise man sees copper, lead, and opportunity. Rust is just a savings account you have to wash your hands to withdraw from."

We walked on, past the manicured family plots, to a section that was a bit wilder, near the fence line where the sumac encroached. A stone here was rough-hewn, a simple boulder with a name chiseled by an amateur hand: SILAS.

"The Miner," Samuel said, chuckling darkly.

"Not a miner," Father Tom corrected. "A Scrapper. Silas the Scrapper."

"He was the man you see pushing the shopping cart full of copper wire," Samuel explained to Elias. "The man stripping the aluminum siding off the condemned garage. To the town, he was a nuisance. A junkie scavenger."

"But he wasn't a junkie," Father Tom said. "He was a believer. He believed that there was value hidden in the ruin. He looked at a rusted 1980 Chevy and saw the catalytic converter, the alternator, the copper core. He saw the potential energy trapped in the waste."

"He spent forty years digging through the trash of the Rust Belt," the Priest continued. "He lived in a trailer with no heat, but he had a shed full of 'treasure'—brass fittings, lead pipes, antique radios. He was saving it. Waiting for the market to turn."

"And?" Elias asked. "Did he strike gold?"

"He found a Barn Find," Samuel said. "A 1963 Corvette, buried under hay in a collapsed barn in Groveland. The Holy Grail. Worth six figures."

"He died the next day," Father Tom said. "Heart attack. He was so excited, his heart just burst. We buried him here. His nephews sold the car and the scrap. They bought jet skis."

"But Silas didn't care," the Priest insisted. "It wasn't about the money, Elias. It was the hunt. It was the refusal to believe that a thing is worthless just because it is broken. He gave this town a dignity it had forgotten, by proving that its trash was worth saving."

Elias touched the rough stone. "Hope," he muttered. "The most dangerous addiction of all."

❧

iv. The Anchor (The Garner Family)

"You can foreclose on a house, but you can't evict a family plot. When you plant four generations in the same dirt, you stop owning the land and start being the land."

We passed a sprawling plot, defined by a low iron rail. It was crowded with stone—a dense city within the city. Dominating the center was a tall, weather-beaten obelisk of white marble, its edges softened by a century of rain.

"Here is your proof, Elias," Samuel said, stopping at the rail. "The Section Corner made flesh."

"Garner," Elias read from the central plinth. "John C. Garner. 1820–1890."

"The man who lost the mill but kept the land," Samuel nodded. "He didn't just build a house; he built a timeline."

Father Tom gestured to the stones radiating out from the patriarch like ripples in a pond. They represented a continuity that was almost startling in our transient age.

"Four generations, Doctor," the Priest said. "It is rare now, but once, it was the rule. Here lies Mary, his daughter, who held the deed when the laws were against her. Here is Lizzie, her daughter, who taught half the county to read. And here is Donald, the great-grandson, who died most recently."

Elias looked at the cluster of headstones that spanned nearly two centuries—spouses, siblings, and children gathered around the original pioneer like a congregation.

"One spot," Elias mused. "One hundred and twenty years of refusing to move."

"They are the anchor," Father Tom said. "The township changed around them. The gravel roads became pavement. The horses became Fords. The farms became subdivisions. But the Garners stayed. There are stories here—feuds, loves, scandals, and saving graces—that would fill a library."

"But we must leave those books closed for now," Samuel said, tipping his cap to the patriarch. "It is enough to know that they held the line."

❧

v. The Dialectic (Frank & Joe)

"Hate is a strong coffee, but it gets cold fast. You can spend thirty years shouting across the fence, but when the lights go out, you're just two old men glad for the company."

We moved to the center of the yard, where two headstones stood side by side, identical in size and shape, like twin beds in a shared room.

FRANK (1940–2018) JOE (1941–2018)

"The Brothers?" I asked.

"The Combatants," Father Tom laughed.

"Frank was the Union Man," Samuel said. "UAW Local 659. A Democrat who thought FDR was the second coming. He believed in the Collective. The Pension. The Strike."

"Joe was the Patriot," the Priest countered. "Small business owner. Tea Party. He believed that if you didn't build it yourself, you didn't own it. He thought taxes were theft and regulations were communism."

"They hated each other," Elias guessed.

"They ate breakfast together every single morning for thirty years," Tom said. "At the diner on Saginaw Street. You could set your watch by the shouting. They argued about Reagan, about

Clinton, about the Wall, about the climate. They turned purple in the face."

"But here is the thing," the Priest said, leaning on Frank's stone. "When Frank had his stroke, and he couldn't drive... who drove him to physical therapy three times a week?"

"Joe," I whispered.

"Joe," Father Tom confirmed. "And when Joe's wife died on Christmas Eve, and he was sitting in that big empty house with a shotgun on his lap, thinking about checking out... who sat with him for three days straight, making coffee and yelling at him about the deficit just to keep him awake?"

"Frank."

"They ended up in the same nursing home," Samuel said. "Room 302. They died a week apart. Frank went first. Joe looked at the empty bed and said, 'Well, there's no one left to educate,' and he let go."

Father Tom looked at Elias.

"You see, Doctor? You look at the news and you see a country at war with itself. You see the polarization. But down here, on the ground? The ideology dissolves. The brotherhood is deeper than the ballot. It is the brotherhood of the bad hip. The brotherhood of the prostate exam. The brotherhood of the fear of the dark."

❧

vi. The Cynic's Doubt

"Cynicism is a raincoat you wear when it isn't raining. It keeps you dry, sure, but it makes you sweat something awful."

Elias stood before the two stones. He looked at the Union Man and the Patriot, resting in the same dirt, fed by the same rain.

"It is a pretty story," Elias said, but his voice lacked its usual bite. "It suggests that our biological vulnerability is the only thing that saves us from our intellectual arrogance."

"Exactly," said Father Tom. "We are all just soft tissue in the end. And soft things need to stick together."

Elias turned away, looking toward the lake. The sun was dipping lower, casting long shadows across the graves.

"Show me more," Elias said quietly. "If we are to tour the museum of false hopes, let us see the whole collection."

"There is one more section," Samuel said, his voice dropping. "The hardest one. The section of the unfulfilled."

"Lead on," Elias said. But he walked slower now, as if the weight of the stories was starting to fill his pockets.

BOOK VII

THE CEMETERY CHRONICLES

(continued)

"A town is like a roof: it isn't the fancy shingles on top that keep you dry; it's the quiet beams underneath that hold the whole thing up. You never notice 'em until one breaks."

— **Samuel Walker,**
Surveyor's Log

i. The Saint of Economy (Mrs. Higgins)

"Wall Street thinks it understands leverage. But the real financial wizardry happens in a kitchen on a Tuesday night, turning one pound of ground beef into dinner for seven people. That isn't cooking; that is alchemy."

We turned from the fraternal argument of the politicos to a modest stone, half-hidden by a sprawling fern. The grass here was trimmed with manicured precision, as if the family came by with scissors rather than a mower.

"Mary Higgins," the stone read. "Beloved Mother."

"You ask for heroes," Father Tom said, wiping his glasses. "Forget the captains of industry. Here lies the strongest logistical mind in Rose Township."

"She was a widow at twenty-nine," the Priest explained. "Her husband died in a press accident at the stamping plant. No pension. No life insurance. Just six kids, the oldest barely ten, and a mortgage on a bungalow on Sherman Street."

"How does a woman feed six mouths on grief?" Elias asked, skeptical.

"She didn't grieve. She didn't have the time," Father Tom said. "She worked the morning shift at the dry cleaners, the lunch shift at the diner, and the night shift scrubbing floors at the elementary school."

"I never saw her sleep," Samuel added, nodding at the grave. "I'd drive past her house at 5:00 a.m. to check a survey line, and the kitchen light was already on. She was packing lunches. Six brown bags, every single day. She washed the clothes. She checked the math homework. She stretched a pound of hamburger to feed seven people with a miracle of breadcrumbs and tomato soup."

"She was the Saint of Economy," Father Tom said. "She never took a handout. She sat in the front pew every Sunday, her coat ten years old but pressed sharp enough to cut paper. She raised three teachers, a nurse, and two mechanics. And when she died, her bank account had exactly enough in it to pay for this stone, with zero left over. She balanced the ledger to the penny."

Elias looked at the modest plot. "A life of grind," he muttered. "A beast of burden."

"A life of sovereignty," Samuel corrected. "She owed nothing to anyone. That is a freedom you and I have never earned, Professor."

❧

ii. The Sensory Exiles (Cal & Bill)

"Just 'cause a man's radio is broken doesn't mean he can't hear the music. Sometimes the guy sitting in the dark sees more than the fellow staring at the sun."

We walked further, where the oak roots buckled the path. Father Tom pointed to two graves that sat near each other, though not side-by-side.

"We had two men in this village," the Priest said, "who lived in half-worlds. This one is 'Silent Cal.' He was born stone deaf. He never heard a bird, a siren, or his mother's voice."

"And he was bitter?" Elias guessed.

"He was observant," the Priest said. "Because he couldn't hear the noise, he watched the motion. He knew it was going to rain before the barometer dropped because he saw the way the maple leaves turned their backs to the wind. He found God in the visual. He used to sit in the back of the church and watch the dust motes dancing in the stained glass light. He told me once, on a notepad, that he thought the dust was the angels moving."

Father Tom walked ten paces to the second stone.

"And this was Bill. 'Blind Bill.' Diabetes took his sight at thirty. But he was the loudest, most joyful man in Holly."

"He sat on his porch on Saginaw Street," Samuel recalled, smiling. "He knew every engine that passed. He'd say, 'That's a Ford V8 running rich,' or 'That's the mail truck, the suspension is squeaking.' He lived in a world of pure sound."

"Why show me this?" Elias asked. "To prove that biology is cruel?"

"To prove that the Spirit is fluid," Father Tom said. "When the door slams shut, the window opens. These men didn't curse the dark or the silence. They inhabited the room that was left to them. They fully occupied the space they had."

iii. The Lost Recruit (Tyler)

"We fold a flag into a triangle and hand it to a mother like it's a fair trade for a son. It's not, but it's the only receipt we got."

We moved toward the edge of the bluff, where a white marble marker stood, distinct from the gray granite around it. It had the sharp, clean lines of a government issue.

TYLER (1998–2019) USMC

"The Patriot?" Elias asked. "Or the Victim?"

"The Recruit," Samuel said, his voice hard. "Tyler. He was a good kid. Strong back. Weak grades. He looked at the town—the closed factories, the minimum wage at the fast-food window, the slow drift of his friends into the opioid fog— and he wanted out."

"He joined the Marines to pay for college," Father Tom said. "He wanted to be an engineer. He wanted to build bridges."

"He died in a training accident," Samuel said. "Stateside. A truck rollover in the Mojave Desert. He never saw a war. He never saw a bridge. His yellow ribbon remains tied around the old oak in front of the school—a fading lash against the bark."

Elias stared at the white stone. This hit close to his theory—the waste of it. The system chewing up the young.

"Unfulfilled potential," Elias said. "The most common resource in the Midwest."

"Perhaps," said Father Tom. "But look at the flag."

A small American flag fluttered in a plastic holder next to the stone. It was fresh.

"The Legion changes it every month," Father Tom said. "And the kids from his class—the ones who stayed, the ones who are drifting—they come here to drink beer on Friday nights. They pour a little out for Tyler. He is their anchor. He is the one who 'went.' His death wasn't fair, Elias. But it wasn't forgotten."

&a.

iv. The Intercessor (The Angel)

"There's a silence so heavy it cracks the pavement. When a cradle stops rocking, even the wind knows enough to shut up and take its hat off."

"And this?" Elias pointed to a tiny stone, no bigger than a shoebox, nestled under the shelter of a weeping cherry tree. It had a single name: GRACE. And a date that spanned only four months.

Father Tom stopped. The air around this stone felt different—heavier, yet still.

"SIDS," the Priest said quietly. "The Thief in the Night. No cause. No symptom. Just a mother waking up on a Tuesday morning to a silence that was too absolute."

Elias stiffened. He turned away, looking out at the lake. His hands clenched in his pockets. This was the raw nerve. This was the "Subtraction" he couldn't calculate.

"I have no theology for this," Father Tom admitted, standing over the tiny marker. "I have no verse that explains a cradle robbed. When I stood here with the parents in the freezing rain, I didn't talk of 'God's Plan.' That is an insult to a mother's grief. I didn't talk of 'Better Places.'"

"Then what did you do?" Elias whispered, his back still turned.

"I just stood there," the Priest said. "We let the tears freeze on our faces. But I tell you this, Doctor: I believe that this small soul, who never spoke a word, who never sinned, who never knew a fear or a doubt, is the most powerful force in this entire yard."

"She is the Intercessor," Samuel said softly. "The pure note."

"When the rest of us are bargaining with God," Father Tom said, "cluttered with our regrets and our politics and our 'Social Contracts,' she just looks up. And the Heavens have to hush."

Elias turned back. He looked at the stone. He looked at the lamb carved into the top, worn smooth by the touch of passing fingers.

He didn't sneer. He didn't quote Hobbes. He didn't argue that she was just biology returned to carbon. For the first time since we left the swamp, the Professor was silent. He took off his hat—a reflex he thought he had subtracted years ago—and held it against his chest.

"The silence," Elias said, his voice cracking, "is very loud here."

&

v. The Bell

"The bell rings for the saint and the sinner alike. It doesn't care about your resume; it just tells you it's time to wash up for supper."

The sun was still high above the tree line across the lake, but the heat had broken. The slanting shadows of the headstones stretched out, touching each other, connecting the Union Man to the Marine, the Saint of Economy to the Angel.

Bong.

The bell in the church tower rang the hour. Six o'clock.

"The day is done," Father Tom said, putting his hand on Elias's shoulder. The Professor didn't flinch.

"The dead have preached their sermon," the Priest said. "They have shown you the labor, the loss, and the love. But they cannot give us the bread to keep us marching. For that, we need the living."

"Where to?" I asked, closing my notebook.

"To the hearth," Samuel said. "To the coffee shop. To the noise of the village. It is time to see if the Professor can handle the chaos of the living as well as he handled the silence of the dead."

BOOK VIII

THE PUBLIC HEARTH

"You cannot keep a fire going with a single log; it needs a neighbor to reflect the heat. Solitude might be peaceful, but it burns out fast. You need friction to keep the room warm."

— **Samuel Walker**,
Field Notes on Domestic Architecture

i. The Economy of Nostalgia

"City folks pay good money for rusted tools to hang on their living room walls. It's a luxury to admire the sharp edge of a tool when you don't have to swing it till your back breaks."

The sun was dropping fast as we left the cemetery gates. The golden hour hit the Village of Holly, turning the brick facades of Battle Alley into a warm, glowing canyon. We drove down the hill, leaving the silence of the dead for the friction of the living.

"You see the shift?" Elias noted, looking out the window at the antique stores and the boutique windows. "We leave the honest rot of the swamp and the honest silence of the grave, and we enter the 'Marketplace of Memory.'"

He pointed a jagged fingernail at a shop window displaying a rusted cast-iron plow and a vintage gas station sign.

"Look at that," Elias sneered. "They sell the tools of their grandfathers as decorations. The plow is no longer for turning earth; it is 'rustic chic.' This is what we have become, Samuel. We don't build anything anymore. We just sell tickets to the museum of when we used to build things."

"It is adaptation," Samuel countered, parking the truck. "The mills closed. The factories moved south. The town could have died. Instead, it reinvented. It peddles charm now. It moves coffee. It survives."

"It is a hollow shell," Elias grumbled. "A service economy built on serving tourists who are looking for a past that never existed."

❧

ii. Battle Alley Brews

"Silence is overrated. A quiet room usually means everyone is mad or everyone is dead. If you want to know if a town is alive, don't check the pulse—listen for the racket."

We walked into "Battle Alley Brews." The bell above the door triggered a wall of sound—the hiss of the espresso machine, the clatter of ceramic, the hum of ten conversations bouncing off the tin ceiling.

It was the "Public Living Room" of the village. At one table, a group of teachers graded papers with red pens like surgeons. At another, a contractor unfolded a blueprint, arguing with a client about the price of lumber. In the corner, a kid still wearing a fast-food visor was now off shift, sleeping with his head on a textbook.

The smell was aggressive and life-affirming: roasted beans, cinnamon, and rain on warm pavement. It was a far cry from the sour, acidic stench of the old Vinegar Works that the old-timers swore still haunted this street on humid days. But today, the air smelled only of five-dollar lattes.

"Noise," Elias winced, putting a hand to his temple. "The chaotic friction of the herd."

"Community," Father Tom corrected. "The sound of people trying to stay connected."

Behind the counter stood Sarah. She was fifty, with hair pulled back in a no-nonsense bun and eyes that missed nothing. She moved with the efficiency of a chaotic system's only engineer—pouring shots, wiping counters, and shouting orders simultaneously.

"Father!" she called out, not stopping her work. "You look like you've been digging ditches. And Samuel... you look like you found a ghost."

She stopped wiping the counter. Her eyes landed on Elias. She took in the mud-stained coat, the wild beard, and the defensive posture. She didn't ask who he was. She knew. In a town of three thousand people, the man who lives in the swamp is not a secret; he is a legend.

"So," Sarah said, leaning over the counter, "the Professor finally comes down from the mountain. Or up from the bog, as it were."

Elias stiffened. "I was not aware I had an audience."

"You don't have an audience, honey," Sarah said, grabbing a clean mug. "You have neighbors. And neighbors talk. I heard you were living off cattails and spite out on Fish Lake Road."

She slammed the mug down.

"Black. No sugar. You look like a man who thinks sugar is a moral failing."

Elias blinked, taken aback by the accuracy. "Precise," he admitted.

❦

iii. The Theology of the Kitchen

"Grief is a heavy sack of rocks. You can drag it alone until your knees give out, or you can let a friend grab a corner. The rocks weigh the same, but the walk gets easier."

We sat in a booth near the back. Sarah brought a pot of dark roast and a plate of scones that steamed on the table. She didn't leave. She stood there with a rag in her hand, looking at Elias like a chef inspecting a delivery of bruised fruit.

"You argue about the 'System,' Doctor," Father Tom said, stirring cream into his cup. "You say the Social Contract is broken. But look at this room. No one commanded these people to be here. No law forced them to share this space. They come because the human animal cannot bear to be alone."

"They come for the caffeine," Elias argued, nursing his mug. "It is a chemical dependency. They are tired, Father. Look at them. The 'Gig Economy' has ground them down. They are here to refuel so they can go back to the treadmill."

"Maybe," Sarah interrupted. "Or maybe they're just hungry."

Elias looked up at her. "Hungry for what, Madam? Distraction?"

"Hungry for proof that they aren't the only ones losing their minds," Sarah said. She pointed the rag at him. "See, that's your problem, Professor. You treat your grief like some rare, expensive wine sipped alone in the dark."

"It is my burden," Elias said coldly.

"It's waste," Sarah countered. "It's leftovers. You're letting it spoil."

She gestured to the room—the teachers, the contractor, the sleeping kid.

"Everyone here has something rotting in their fridge. That woman? Husband has Alzheimer's. The kid in the corner? Living in his car. But they show up. They put it in the stew. They share the load."

She looked Elias dead in the eye.

"You hiding in that swamp isn't noble. It's just hoarding. You're taking all that pain, all that experience, and you're letting it go moldy when you could be using it to feed someone else who's starving."

Elias stared at her. He had expected a theological argument from the Priest or a structural one from the Surveyor. He had not expected a culinary critique of his soul.

"You possess a brutal bedside manner, Madam," Elias said softly.

"I'm a mother," Sarah shrugged. "I don't have time to garnish the truth. Dinner is at seven. The farmhouse. You're coming."

"I..." Elias started to protest.

"It wasn't a question," she said, and walked away to steam milk for a latte.

❦

iv. The Private Sanctuary

"Vinyl siding covers a multitude of sins, but brick tells the truth. An old house doesn't echo when you yell because the walls are already full of a hundred years of conversations."

We followed her instructions. We drove out of the village proper.

"Turn right on Hensell," I said, checking the GPS.

"The Old Indian Trail," Samuel corrected, turning the wheel without looking at the sign. "The county renamed it in the twenties, but the ridge didn't change."

We drove down the winding gravel to the place where the "Public Hearth" gave way to the "Private Sanctuary."

The farmhouse was a brick fortress built generations ago, sitting on a rise that overlooked ten acres of pasture and a winding creek. It was the antithesis of the "Ghost Subdivision" from yesterday. This house had deep roots. The ivy clinging to the bricks was older than the Professor. "It still needed work when we bought it," Sarah told us later. "But the owners before us had already pulled it back from the brink. They were the ones who fixed the blown-out windows and chased out the raccoons. We just took it the rest of the way."

I stepped onto the porch. The third board gave a loud, complaining squeak under my boot.

"Watch that step," Sarah called from inside, unseen. "My husband swore he fixed that squeak ten years ago. The house is stubborn."

We walked into the kitchen, and the chaos hit us again—but this was a different frequency. This was the chaos of the family.

I crossed the threshold into the dining room, my boot catching on a ridge in the floor where the wide-plank old-growth pine was scarred with deep, black char marks that climbed the base-boards and scorched the heavy panels of the doors. "The caretakers," Samuel whispered, "tried to burn the history out of the house; Sarah had sanded the wounds smooth but refused to hide them, claiming the scars proved the house had won the argument."

The back door slammed. Muddy cleats clat-tered on the hardwood. Backpacks hit the floor with the heavy thud of physics textbooks.

"Mom! Is the chicken done?"

The Son entered—sixteen, all knees and elbows, smelling of grass stains and adolescence. Behind him was The Friend, a lanky boy grinning at a joke on his phone. Emily, the daughter, sat at the island counter, ignoring them, lost in a thick novel, spinning a strand of hair around her finger.

They stopped when they saw us. The Priest. The Surveyor. The stranger with the wild beard.

"Guests," Sarah announced, pulling a roasting pan from the oven. The smell of rosemary and chicken fat filled the room, primal and heavy. "Set the extra places. Use the good napkins."

❧

v. The Collision

"The only place you'll find perfect order is a grave-yard. A dinner table should be a mess of crumbs, spilled milk, and arguments. That's how you know the food was good."

We sat at the long wooden table. Elias was wedged between The Son and Father Tom. The Solitary, who had spent three years listening only to frogs and his own dark thoughts, was suddenly in the crossfire of teenage dinner conversation.

They didn't treat him like a fragile intellectual. They passed the potatoes.

"So, you live in the swamp?" the Son asked, piling mash onto his plate. "Like... near the gamelands?"

"I live in the Fen," Elias corrected stiffly. "Near the biodiversity preservation zone."

"Cool," the boy said. "I saw a coyote out there last week. Massive. Size of a wolf. You see any?"

"I... I have heard them," Elias admitted.

"Pass the butter," Emily said, not looking up from her book.

"Put the book down, Em," Sarah commanded. "We have a Professor at the table."

"What do you teach?" Emily asked Elias, assessing him with sharp, intelligent eyes.

"I... I used to teach Political Science," Elias stammered. "The study of power and systems."

"Did you teach that the system is broken?" Emily asked. "Because it feels pretty broken."

Elias looked at Samuel. Samuel smiled into his wine glass.

"I taught," Elias said slowly, "that systems are fragile. And that entropy—the tendency toward disorder—is the natural state of the universe."

"That's why we have chores," Sarah interrupted, slamming a bowl of green beans on the table. "Entropy is just what happens when you stop scrubbing the pot. The universe might be falling apart, Professor, but in this kitchen, we wash up after we eat."

Elias looked at the plate before him. Roast chicken. Steaming potatoes. Green beans from the garden outside. It was a meal of aggressive normalcy.

He picked up his fork. He looked at the chaos around him—the laughing boys, the reading girl, the commanding mother, the praying priest.

"It is... noisy," Elias whispered to me.

"Yes," I whispered back. "It's the opposite of Zero."

Elias took a bite. For the first time in years, he wasn't consuming his own bitterness. He was just eating dinner.

BOOK IX

THE DISCOURSE OF

THE SURVEYOR

"Any dead fish can float downstream; the current does all the work for you. If you see something swimming against the flow, you know it's alive. Struggle isn't a tragedy, son; it's the only proof of life we have."

— **Samuel Walker,**
Final Entry, The Survey of Rose Township

i. The Twilight Walk

"Folks mourn the sunset like the light died. The light didn't die; it just moved on to wake up somebody else. Darkness isn't an ending; it's just a shift change."

The dinner was done. The "Private Sanctuary" had done its work—feeding the bodies and warming the room against the coming night. The teenagers retreated to the basement, their laughter muffled by the floorboards, a subterranean rumble of the future continuing its chaotic business.

We—the Elders and the Witness—stepped out onto the back porch.

The sun had fallen behind the ridge, leaving the sky a bruised purple, fading to black. The air was still and smelled of damp grass, woodsmoke, and the specific, mineral scent of the Buckhorn Creek, which wound through the bottom of the property and fed the mighty Shiawassee further downstream.

"The light is failing," Elias noted, buttoning his coat. "The cycle returns to darkness. It is the only reliable promise."

"The light is moving," Samuel corrected. "It is hitting the Pacific now. It never fails, Elias; it just travels."

Samuel grabbed his hickory pole. He didn't look tired. The dinner seemed to have sharpened him, as if the noise of the family had refueled his tank.

"Walk with me," he said. "To the water. We began this journey in the drought of the roadside. We should end it at the source."

&

ii. The Watershed Sermon

"The swamp thinks it's the end of the world because it's stuck. But the river knows better. It takes the mud, scrubs it on the rocks, and sends it downstream. Nothing is wasted, not even the dirt."

We walked down the sloping lawn, our boots slick with dew. We passed the garden where Sarah grew the beans we had just eaten. We passed the barn, settling into the earth with the dignity of a retired general.

We stopped at the riverbank. The Buckhorn was not a mighty torrent here; it was a dark, steady muscle moving north, carrying the runoff of the township toward the distant Saginaw Bay.

Samuel planted his staff in the mud. He looked at the water, black and glossy as oil in the starlight.

"You asked me in the Fen about the 'Point' of it all," Samuel said to Elias. "You asked why we should build a porch that will rot, or love a child who will leave, or govern a town that is past its prime."

"I did," Elias said. "And I am still waiting for the math."

"The math is the Current," Samuel said.

He pointed upstream, toward the darkness of the wetlands.

"This water bleeds from the Fen, Elias. It issues from your swamp. It is distilled through the rot and the decay. But it doesn't stay there. It moves. It joins the creek. It turns the wheel. It waters the corn. It reaches the Great Lakes. It evaporates and becomes the rain that falls on the graves of our grandfathers."

"This is the Active Principle," Samuel declared, his voice rising over the sound of the crickets. "It is the spirit that knows no insulated spot. There is no 'Zero,' Doctor. Even in your decay, you are feeding the soil. Even in your silence, you are defining the noise."

"We do not live to 'win,'" Samuel said, looking at the stars reflecting in the water. "We do not live to 'fix' the system. We live to be part of the flow. To take the water from the upstream generation, filter it through our own suffering, and pass it downstream to the boys in that basement."

"To stop the flow," Samuel whispered, "is the only sin. To become a stagnant pool. That is what you have done in the marsh. You have dammed yourself up."

❧

iii. The Witness (Jim's Epiphany)

"Drifting isn't freedom; it's just drowning slowly. If you want to matter, you have to be a rock in the stream. Make the water bend around you for a change."

I stood back, listening. For days, I had been the scribe, the drifter, the man waiting for a gig. I had looked at the Ghost Subdivision and seen my own future—a life of temporary leases and peeling siding.

But standing there, smelling the river and the smoke, I realized Samuel was talking to me.

The "Drift" I felt wasn't freedom. It was just stagnation. I had been floating on the surface, terrified to put my feet down because I was afraid of the mud. But the mud was where the life was. The mud was where Mrs. Higgins stood. It was where Frank and Joe stood.

I looked at the river. I realized that I didn't want to be a ghost anymore. I wanted to be a rock in the stream—something the water had to move around, something that changed the current, even just a little.

iv. The Solitary's Concession

"The Professor thought he could fix his life by throwing everything out. But you can't calculate the size of a room if you knock down all the walls. The pain is just the corner post; without it, the roof falls in."

Elias stood silent for a long time. He watched a firefly blink on, then off, then on again—a tiny, biological Morse code against the void.

He bent down. He picked up a stone from the bank. It was smooth, worn by ten thousand years of friction.

He weighed it in his hand. The Academic weighing the evidence.

"I cannot promise you, Samuel," Elias said quietly, "that I will leave the cabin. The silence there... it is a habit now. And I am an old dog who is fond of his own mange."

He looked back at the farmhouse. The kitchen window was a rectangle of yellow warmth in the dark hill. He could see Sarah's silhouette moving past the sink.

"But," Elias continued, "I will admit... the walls of my logic were not as watertight as I thought. The damp got in. And today..." he looked at the stone, "...the light got in."

"I will not say I have found Faith," Elias said, his voice rough. "That is a bridge too far. But I will say that the data set is... incomplete. The equation of the Zero does not account for the woman who bakes six loaves of bread for a stranger."

He tossed the stone into the river.

Plonk.

No dramatic splash. Just a small, wet sound consumed by the river. The stone settled on the bottom, joining the millions of other stones that made the bed.

"I am part of the watershed," Elias whispered. "Whether I like it or not."

&

v. The Benediction

"Weeds are persistent, but iron is stubborn. We don't drive the stake expecting it to last forever. We do it just to tell the rust it is going to have a fight on its hands."

"That is enough," Samuel said, satisfied. "We do not need a convert, Elias. We just need a neighbor."

Samuel pulled his pole from the mud.

"The Excursion is done," the Surveyor announced. "The traverse is closed. We have walked the loop from the Road to the Ruin, to the Swamp, to the Hill, to the Hearth, and back to the River."

"And what did we find?" I asked.

Samuel looked at me. He looked at the sky, where the constellation of Orion was just beginning to hunt above the treeline.

"We found that the rust is real," Samuel said. "But the root is deeper."

He turned back toward the house.

"Come," he said. "Sarah is making coffee. And tomorrow, Jim, you have a story to write. Not about how the world is ending. But about how it persists."

We turned our backs on the dark water and walked up the hill, toward the lights of the farmhouse, three men walking on the uneven ground of the American Midwest, bound by the gravity of the earth and the stubborn, holy work of carrying on.

&

"We walked the whole loop—from the ruin to the river—and found that the Zero is a lie. Hope is not a bird with feathers; it's a beam with bolts. It holds the roof up when the snow gets heavy. Our job is not to fix the world permanently; it's just to keep the rain out for one more night. The survey is done. The rest is just maintenance."

> — **Samuel Walker**,
> *Final Entry, Field Log 2026*

END NOTES

A Field Guide to the Original

Since I began sharing drafts of *The Excursion: A Modern American Retelling*, the question I am asked most frequently is this: *"Do I need to read William Wordsworth's original poem to understand this book?"*

The short answer is: No.

The long answer is: You should, but you probably won't, and I don't blame you.

Wordsworth's *The Excursion*, published in 1814, is a massive, sprawling epic. It runs for nine books and consists of over 9,000 lines of blank verse. It is philosophical, dense, and moves at the speed of a contemplative hike in the nineteenth century—which is to say, very slowly. It was controversial in its time and remains daunting in ours.

However, the reason I wrote this retelling is that the *ghosts* inside that dense poem are startlingly modern. Wordsworth was writing at a moment of terrified transition. The Industrial Revolution was tearing apart the English countryside; the political hopes of the French Revolution had collapsed into violence; and the rural poor were being displaced by economic forces they couldn't control.

Does that sound familiar?

When I looked at my own backyard in Oakland County, Michigan—at the "Rust Belt" landscape of shuttered factories, polarized politics, and the gig economy—I realized we are living through the exact same anxieties.

So, I wrote this book to ease the burden. I wanted to extract the timeless architecture of Wordsworth's argument and rebuild it using modern materials: vinyl siding, fentanyl, and foreclosure signs.

For those curious about how the translation works, or for the students among you who want to see the gears turning, here is a guide to the changes I made.

THE CAST: ARCHETYPES REIMAGINED

The Wanderer: Samuel Walker (The Surveyor)

In 1814, the hero was a Peddler—a man who walked the countryside selling goods and gathering wisdom. In 2026, a peddler doesn't make much sense. I changed him to a **Land Surveyor**. Why? Because a surveyor deals in "The Grid." He looks for the "Iron Pin" buried deep in the earth. This fit perfectly with the theme that truth is objective and buried beneath the surface rot.

The Solitary: Dr. Elias Thorne (The Cynic)

Wordsworth's "Solitary" was a man who lost his family and then lost his faith in the French Revolution. Today, our disillusionment isn't usually about French royalty; it's about the American System. Elias is a former Political Science professor who believed in the "Social Contract" until a drunk driver (and a failed legal system) proved to him that chaos rules. He represents the modern urge to withdraw into a silo of despair.

The Pastor: Father Tom Cole

Wordsworth's Pastor was a country parson in the Church of England. I made Father Tom a Catholic priest at **St. Jude's** (the patron saint of hopeless cases) because the Catholic emphasis on the "Communion of Saints" provided a strong counter-argument to Elias's individualism.

The Poet: Jim Miller (The Gig Worker)

In the original, the narrator is simply "The Poet," a largely passive observer. I wanted our narrator to have skin in the game. Jim is a "Millennial Drifter," paralyzed by the instability of the modern economy. He isn't just watching; he is trying to figure out how to survive.

BOOK I: THE RUINED COTTAGE vs. THE GHOST SUBDIVISION

This is the most direct translation in the book. Wordsworth's famous "Ruined Cottage" tells the story of Margaret, whose husband Robert joins the army out of poverty, leaving her to decline and die in their decaying home.

I transposed this to a **"Ghost Subdivision"**—one of those developments stalled by the 2008 crash.

- **Robert the Weaver** became **Rob the Carpenter**, who leaves not for war, but for the **Bakken Oil Fields** in North Dakota.
- **Margaret** became **Maggie**, who dies not of a broken heart in a cottage, but of heart failure ("Waiting") in a foreclosure wrapped in Tyvek.

The tragedy remains identical: macro-economic forces destroying the domestic sanctuary.

BOOKS II–IV: THE ROCKY VALE vs. THE FEN

Wordsworth placed his Solitary in a dramatic, rocky valley. I moved Elias to a **fen** (a peat-forming wetland) off Fish Lake Road.

- **Why the Fen?** A fen is biologically fascinating—it preserves bone but dissolves soft tissue. It is the perfect metaphor for Elias's nihilism. He thinks he is stripping life down to the bone ("The Subtraction").
- **The Debate:** In the original, the debate is largely theological. I shifted it to be more civic. Samuel argues that **"Hope is a disci-**

pline." This is a crucial update. We are not waiting for divine intervention; we are doing the work of maintenance.

BOOKS V–VII: THE CHURCHYARD vs. THE LEDGER

This is the heart of the poem. The group tours the cemetery to prove to the cynic that life has meaning. I kept the structure but updated the "Case Studies" to reflect American archetypes.

- **The Jacobite & The Hanoverian – Frank & Joe:** Wordsworth described two enemies from a civil war buried together. I changed this to a **Union Democrat** and a **Tea Party Republican**. It allows us to address our current polarization and show that, in the end, we help each other to the bathroom in the nursing home. Biology trumps ideology.

- **The Miner – Silas the Scrapper:** Wordsworth had a man searching for gold. I changed him to a "Scrapper" collecting copper and junk. It's a very specific Rust Belt activity—finding value in the wreckage.

- **The Matron – Mrs. Higgins:** The "Saint of Economy" who raised six kids on minimum wage is a direct tribute to the endurance of the working-class mother.

- **The Unrequited Lover – Ethan:** In 1814, a young man dies of a broken heart. In 2026, he dies of **fentanyl**. It captures the same sensitivity and the desire to "stop the noise" (or close the aperture) of a harsh world.

BOOK VIII: THE PARSONAGE vs. THE PUBLIC HEARTH

Wordsworth uses this book to critique the Factory System. I used it to critique the **"Economy of Nostalgia."** Elias points out that the town now sells "rustic chic" decor (old plows, saws) to tourists—we sell the memory of work rather than the work itself.

We move from the abstract debate to **"Battle Alley Brews"** and then the **Farmhouse**. The introduction of Sarah (The Matron) provides the feminine, practical counter-weight to the men's abstract philosophizing. She doesn't argue; she cooks dinner.

BOOK IX: THE LAKE vs. THE WATERSHED

The original poem ends on a boat on a lake, with a heavy emphasis on Pantheism (God in Nature).

I moved the finale to the **Buckhorn Creek** to focus on the **Watershed**. The "Active Principle" isn't just a spiritual vibe; it is a hydrological fact. The water flows from Elias's swamp, cleanses itself, and feeds the farm.

The Resolution:

In the original, the Solitary is not magically "cured." He simply agrees to spend another day with his friends. I kept this quiet ending. Elias tosses a stone into the river, admitting his data was "incomplete." He doesn't find God, but he finds his Neighbor.

And really, that is the point of *The Excursion*. We don't have to solve the universe. We just have to agree to walk each other home.

—*Peter James Stouffer*
Holly, Michigan, 2026

THE EXCURSION:

A READER'S COMPANION

A Guide for The Public Hearth

NOTE TO THE HOST

In *The Excursion*, the "Public Hearth" (Battle Alley Brews) and the "Private Sanctuary" (Sarah's Kitchen) are places where friction creates warmth. Consider setting the mood for your discussion by serving something simple and grounding—strong coffee, roasted root vegetables, or fresh bread. As Sarah notes, "The universe might be falling apart... but in this kitchen, we wash up after we eat" (Book VIII, v).

PART I: DISCUSSION QUESTIONS

I. The Architecture of Hope vs. The Comfort of Zero

The central conflict of the book is not a physical battle, but a structural one between Samuel (The Surveyor) and Elias (The Solitary).

- **The Discipline of Hope:** Samuel argues that "Hope is not an emotion. Hope is a discipline. It is the stubborn, grinding work of locating the coordinates of dignity in the middle of the disaster" (Book IV, ii). Do you agree that hope is an act of will rather than a feeling? How does this definition change how we view optimism?

- **The Seduction of the Zero:** Elias moves to the Fen to perform "The Subtraction," stripping his life down to see if anything remains. Have you ever felt the temptation of the "Zero"—the desire to simply stop participating in a broken system? Why is Elias's nihilism described as "seductive" and "peaceful" (Book III, iv)?

II. The Geography of the Soul

The book suggests that "The geography of this poem is real" and that the land itself shapes the characters.

- **The Ghost Subdivision vs. The Iron Pin:** The story begins in a foreclosure where the "math was wrong" (Book I, i) and ends at the "Iron Pin" that hasn't moved since the 1830s (Book IV, i). In your own life, what are the "vinyl" structures (things that rot/fade) and what are the "Iron Pins" (things that hold the line)?

- **The Fen and The Watershed:** Elias believes the swamp is a place where things go to die/dissolve. Samuel argues it is part of a "Watershed" that filters water for the downstream generation (Book IX, ii). Does this shift in perspective—from "stagnant pool" to "active current"—change how you view your own hardships?

III. Community and Polarization

The visit to the Cemetery (Book VI) serves as a counter-argument to modern political division.

- **Frank & Joe:** The story of the Union Man and the Tea Party Patriot suggests that "Biology trumps ideology." They argued for thirty years but cared for each other in the end (Book VI, v). Is this kind of relationship still possible in today's polarized climate? Does the book suggest we need *less* politics or just *more* recognition of our shared "soft tissue"?

- **The Saint of Economy:** Mrs. Higgins is described as having "sovereignty" because she owed nothing to anyone and "balanced the ledger" (Book VII, i). Why does Samuel view her life of grinding labor as a triumph rather than a tragedy?

IV. The Role of the Witness

The narrator, Jim, is a "Millennial Drifter" paralyzed by the "noise" of the Gig Economy.

- **Drifting vs. Flowing:** By the river, Jim realizes that "Drifting isn't freedom; it's just drowning slowly" (Book IX, iii). What is the difference between "drifting" (lack of connection) and being part of the "current" (the active principle)?

- **The "Noticer":** In the cemetery, Ethan the photographer dies because he was a "Noticer" who felt the world too intensely (Book VI, ii). Jim is also a "scribe" and observer. Is the role of the artist/writer in this book viewed as a burden or a necessity?

PART II: DEEP DIVE
THE NATURE OF ARGUMENT

The characters in *The Excursion* do not speak in "chatter"; they speak in "orations."

- **Style as Substance:** How did the formal, philosophical style of the dialogue affect your reading? Did it make the characters feel distant, or did it give their arguments more weight?

- **The Interruptions:** Sarah (The Matron) is the only character who successfully interrupts the philosophical debate, not with logic, but with dinner (Book VIII, v). Does the book ultimately side with the Philosophers (Samuel/Elias) or the Doers (Sarah/Mrs. Higgins)?

PART III: FROM THE KITCHEN
MRS. HIGGINS' "MIRACLE STEW"
(The Saint of Economy's Special)

In *The Excursion* (Book VII, i), Samuel describes how Mrs. Higgins could "stretch a pound of hamburger to feed seven people with a miracle of breadcrumbs and tomato soup." This recipe is a tribute to that "alchemy" of the Rust Belt kitchen— a dish that is humble, hearty, and refuses to let anyone go hungry.

Yields: Dinner for 7 (if you serve it with bread)

Prep time: 15 minutes | **Cook time:** 1 hour

The "Miracle" Ingredients:

- 1 lb ground beef (80/20 is best for flavor)

- 1.5 cups dry breadcrumbs (the stretcher)

- 1 egg, beaten

- 1 onion, diced

- 3 large potatoes, peeled and cubed

- 4 carrots, sliced into coins

- 2 cans (10.75 oz) condensed tomato soup

- 2 soup cans of water

- 1 tsp salt & 1/2 tsp black pepper

- 1 tbsp Worcestershire sauce (the "secret")

The Method:

1. **The Stretch:** In a mixing bowl, combine the ground beef, breadcrumbs, egg, salt, and pepper. Mix until just combined. Roll into small meatballs (about the size of a walnut). *Note: The breadcrumbs absorb the juices, doubling the volume of the meat.*

2. **The Sear:** In a large heavy-bottomed pot (or Dutch oven), brown the meatballs in batches. You don't need to cook them through, just get a crust on them. Remove and set aside.

3. **The Base:** In the fat rendered from the beef, sauté the onions until soft. Add the potatoes and carrots.

4. **The Alchemy:** Pour in the tomato soup and water. Scrape the bottom of the pot to get the browned bits (the "fond"). Stir in the Worcestershire sauce.

5. **The Simmer:** Return the meatballs to the pot. Bring to a boil, then reduce heat to low. Cover and simmer for 45 minutes, or until the potatoes are tender and the sauce has thickened.

6. **Serve:** Ladle into bowls. As Mrs. Higgins would do, serve with a slice of buttered bread to soak up the "dividend" of the sauce.

PART IV: A CONVERSATION WITH PETER JAMES STOUFFER

Q: In the End Notes, you write that "the geography of this poem is real." Why did you choose Rose Township and Holly as the stage for this retelling?

A: I have lived in Rose Township for over twenty-five years. I love this land—the glacial moraines, the lakes, and the village of Holly nearby. While the geography in the book is largely accurate, I did take some liberties to make the story flow; in reality, the Village is adjacent to the Township, not inside it. But I wanted to create an "idealized" Midwestern town—a place that feels specific enough to be real, but universal enough to represent the entire Rust Belt experience.

Q: The dialogue in *The Excursion* is very distinct. The characters don't speak in casual slang; they speak in what you call "orations." Was it difficult to write in that voice while dealing with modern grit?

A: It was certainly a challenge. It isn't how real people talk at the grocery store, but I wasn't trying to capture realism; I was trying to capture the Archetype. When I looked at Wordsworth's original—and even Shakespeare—I realized their characters spoke at an elevated level to match the weight of their souls. That kept me motivated. I wanted the Surveyor and the Solitary to sound like "spirits inhabiting a condition," not just neighbors chatting over a fence.

Q: The narrator, Jim, is a "Millennial Drifter" struggling to find his footing in the gig economy. Is he based on your own experience?

A: Definitely not. I come from an engineering background and have spent my career running mid-sized companies—very different from Jim's artistic paralysis! But I have children, and I watch the children of my close friends. Jim is a blend of their generation. I wanted to capture that specific anxiety of being "over-educated and under-employed," drifting through a world that doesn't offer the same solid ground previous generations stood on.

Q: The characters in the cemetery—the Union Man, the Patriot, the Scrapper—feel incredibly specific. Are they based on real people?

A: All of them are semi-based on people I have known over the years. You can't make up a character like Silas the Scrapper or Mrs. Higgins without seeing that kind of resilience firsthand. But as for who they really are? I'll never tell. The names on the stones have been changed to protect the stubborn.

Q: If there is one thing you hope readers take away from this retelling, what would it be?

A: Look at the water. The poem begins in the first line with "drying creeks"—a landscape of drought and scarcity. It ends with a flowing river that feeds the Great Lakes. The question is: Where did the water come from? It didn't rain. The water came from the Fen. It came from the ground, from *within*. I want readers to realize that hope and perseverance aren't things that fall from the sky; they are things we have to dig for, right here in the mud.

CLOSING REFLECTION

"The Survey is Done"

At the end of the book, Samuel states: "Our job is not to fix the world permanently; it's just to keep the rain out for one more night" (Book IX, Field Log).

- **Group Discussion:** If you had to identify one "shingle" you are responsible for patching in your own community—one small act of maintenance—what would it be?